IMPRINT

A part of Macmillan Children's Publishing Group, a division of Macmillan Publishing Group, LLC

ABOUT THIS BOOK

The illustrations started as original pencil drawings, which were then scanned and digitally colored in Adobe Photoshop. After the color foundation was set, textures were layered on top to convey the look of wood or stone, achieving a finish that makes you feel as if you can touch Tomo's world. The text was set in Futura, and the display types are Kabel and Soko. The book was edited by Erin Stein. The production was supervised by Raymond Ernesto Colón, and the production editor was Ilana Worrell.

Library of Congress Cataloging-in-Publication Data is available.
ISBN 978-1-250-08546-7

Our books may be purchased in bulk for promotional, educational, or business use. Please contact your local bookseller or the Macmillan Corporate and Premium Sales Department at (800) 221-7945 ext. 5442 or by e-mail at MacmillanSpecialMarkets@macmillan.com.

Imprint logo designed by Amanda Spielman

First Edition—2017
1 3 5 7 9 10 8 6 4 2

mackids.com

Books are meant to love and hold. Buy or borrow; never steal. Heed these words or else one day, you'll become a whale's next meal!

For Mom and Dad —T.L.

TREVOR LAI

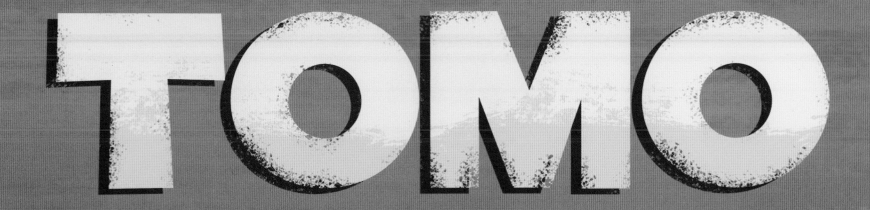

TOMO
TAKES FLIGHT

New York

One sunny morning, Tomo looks up at the sky. He wonders what it would be like to fly as high as the clouds.

"Remember your homework," his father says. "Catch one fish a day! Your grandfather will help you while I'm gone."

Tomo asks his grandfather for a bucket. "I need it for fishing."

"This is my lucky bucket. It always catches a lot," Grandpa says with a smile.

Tomo invents a fishing machine.
It will fish all day
while he goes exploring.

Captain helps Tomo find his best friend.
"Hi, Maya! What are you up to?"

"I'm trying to figure out what kind of
animal made these tracks," she replies.

Tomo says, "Let's look in my great-grandfather's journal for a new
adventure. If you join me, I'll help you solve that mystery, too!"

Maya thinks for a moment. "Okay, it's a deal!"

The friends head to their
secret clubhouse to check
out the Adventure Journal.
It's full of quests to go on
and inventions to build.

Tomo finds a drawing of a flying machine,
but some of the details are missing.

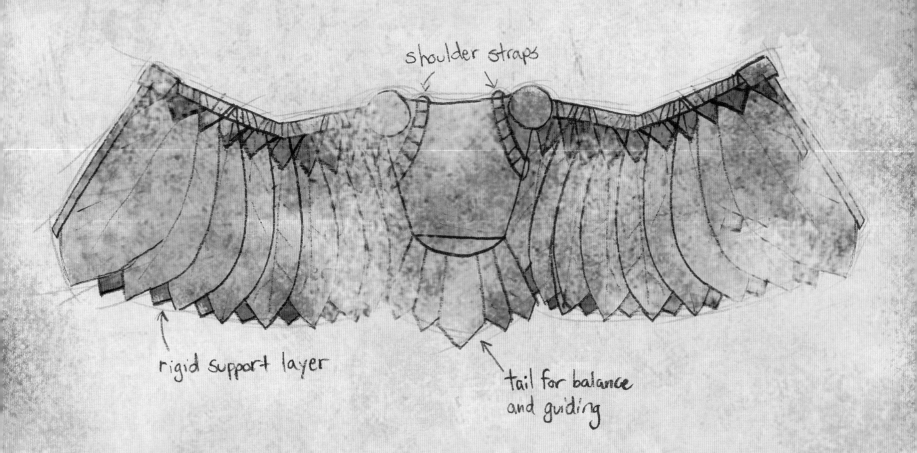

"If I build this, I'll be able to fly!" he says.
"And from the sky, I can look for the animal that left those tracks!"

With Maya and Captain's help, Tomo gathers the materials he needs. Tomo guesses how to construct the flying machine's wings.

When it's finished, Tomo straps on his invention and takes a running leap.

Tomo tries . . .

and tries . . .

but the machine doesn't fly.

"I don't know how to make it work," Tomo admits.

"Birds know how to fly best!" says Maya.
"You just need to build your machine to work like a bird's wings."

I have built a bird sanctuary for several species of rare and endangered birds discovered during my adventures.

sanctuary in dense forest

The boka bird has a beautiful morning song that can carry on for minutes at a time.

brilliant blue wattle

"Look—the Adventure Journal has notes about a rare bird called the boka bird," says Tomo. "There's a map to a bird sanctuary right here on Half-Moon Bay!"

Tomo, Maya, and Captain follow the map into the forest.
"These tracks look like the ones you saw before," says Tomo.

"There's a feather!" notices Maya. "And another one!"
Captain has the smartest nose on the island.
He sniffs the ground, leading the friends
to a bird's broken nest.

"Look, up in the sky," says Tomo. "It's a boka!"
"The wings are beautiful," says Maya.

"Wow, if I had wings like that, I could definitely fly," Tomo replies.
Captain agrees. "Woof! Woof!"

Tomo quickly builds a bird-watching
tower, then climbs up to carefully
study the boka bird as it flies.

He draws the boka's wings and tail
to better understand how it works.

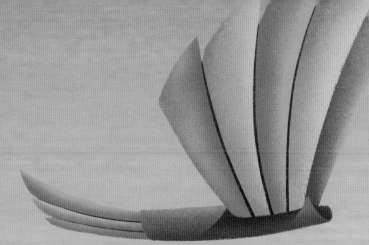

"Why do you think it's carrying sticks in its mouth?" asks Maya.

"I don't know, but I think I do know how to build my machine!" Tomo declares.

Tomo rebuilds his flying machine with Maya and Captain.

"Wow, you look just like a bird!" Maya laughs.

Tomo says, "I hope I can fly like one, too."

He runs and flaps his wings
as fast as he can. Tomo feels
his feet lifting off the ground.
"I'm flying!" he shouts.

Tomo flies higher and higher, until he finds himself wing-to-wing with the boka.

Suddenly the bird dives toward the ground. Tomo makes an emergency landing.

"Are you okay?" Maya asks.

"I'm fine, but I do need to work on my landing," Tomo replies. "Look—there are two young chicks here!"

"The boka bird is a mother!" cheers Maya. "Her babies must have fallen out of the broken nest."

"You're right. Like most birds, the boka builds a nest high up in a tree to keep its babies safe," says Tomo, checking the Adventure Journal.

"We've got to help the mother build a new nest," says Maya.

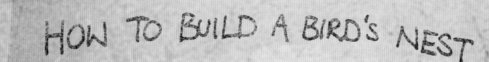

leaves

mud

branches

HOW TO BUILD A BIRD'S NEST

Things you'll need:

① Long, flexible plant stems or branches to shape the bird's nest.

② Moss and mud to help the pieces of the nest stick together.

The friends quickly build a new
nest out of branches, moss, and mud.
Tomo uses his flying machine to
find a safe treetop home.

The mother boka inspects it carefully
and then settles into her new home with her chicks.

As the boka glides back into the sky, Tomo joins her for an aerial tour of Half-Moon Bay—where his father is returning to shore. Time to go!

Tomo checks his Fish-o-Matic invention.
It caught four sea stars, two lobsters,
and luckily, one fish!

Tomo returns the bucket to his grandfather just as his father arrives home.

"Looks like you finished your homework!" his dad says.
"Yup," replies Tomo. "Maya and I have one more
thing to do. Be right back!"

In their clubhouse, Tomo and Maya add
the boka's feather to their collection.
"We helped the birds and finished another quest in the
Adventure Journal," says Tomo. "Plus, I built my flying machine!"

"It was a great adventure," says Maya, "but next time . . ."

"... I want to fly, too!"

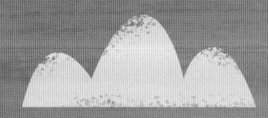

AUTHOR'S NOTE

As a child, just like Tomo and Maya, I always loved exploring and always loved animals. When I grew up and learned about endangered species—and species that had become extinct—it made me very sad that there are some animals no one will ever encounter again. One of my inspirations for *Tomo Takes Flight* was the fundamental idea that while we are exploring and inventing, we should also use our talents to care for animals and nature. In fact, the boka bird in this book was inspired by the real-life kōkako bird, which is an endangered species. If you want to help, look for ways to support your local parks or nature conservation groups. And be nice to every animal you meet on your adventures!